The Sunflower Sword
Sperring, Mark
AR Quiz No. 141847 EN Fiction
? IL: **LG** - BL: **3.6** - AR Pts: **0.5**
? AR Quiz Types: **RP**
? Rating: ★★⯪☆

For my friend Rob. M.S.

To Seb for all your support and for bringing me cups of tea. Love M.L.

First American edition published in 2011 by Andersen Press USA, an imprint of Andersen Press Ltd.
www.andersenpressusa.com

First published in Great Britain in 2010 by Andersen Press Ltd., 20 Vauxhall Bridge Road, London SW1V 2SA.
Published in Australia by Random House Australia Pty., Level 3, 100 Pacific Highway, North Sydney, NSW 2060.

Text copyright © Mark Sperring, 2010. Illustration copyright © Miriam Latimer, 2010.
Jacket illustrations copyright © Miriam Latimer, 2010.

Distributed in the United States and Canada by
Lerner Publishing Group, Inc.
241 First Avenue North, Minneapolis, MN 55401 U.S.A.
www.lernerbooks.com

Color separated in Switzerland by Photolitho AG, Zürich. Printed and bound in Singapore by Tien Wah Press.

Library Cataloging-in-Publication Data available.
ISBN 978-0-7613-7486-2
1 — TWP — 9/8/10

The Sunflower SWORD

MARK SPERRING

MIRIAM LATIMER

ANDERSEN PRESS USA

Once there was a land filled with fire and smoke and endless fighting, where knights fought dragons and dragons fought knights, and that was the way it had always been.

In this land, there lived a knight
who wanted to
be big like
the other
knights and fight
like the other
knights and have a sword
like the other knights.

But his mother
said he couldn't.

"Why do you want a sword?" she asked.
"To whoosh and swoosh in the air," smiled the little knight.

"Hmmm," said his mother,
and she hurried off to find . . .

. . . a sunflower!

"Well," sighed the little knight,
"I suppose I could pretend it's a sword."

Then he **whooshed** and **swooshed** it,

just to see how well

it **whooshed** and **swooshed.**

It whooshed

and swooshed very well.

"But," said the little
knight, "it won't be any
good for fighting dragons."
"No," sighed his mother,
"I don't suppose it will,
but keep it anyway."

So the little knight trundled up Dragon Hill, a place where only the **biggest**, **bravest** knights ever went. He played happily all day.

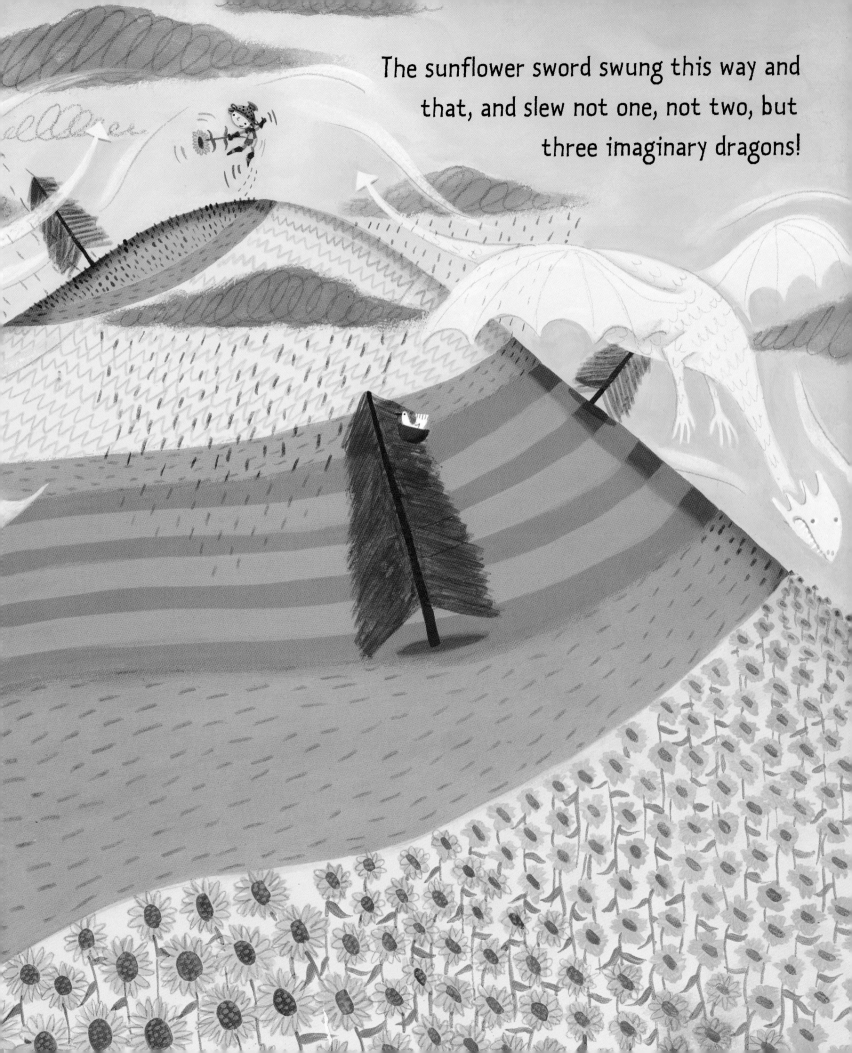

The sunflower sword swung this way and that, and slew not one, not two, but three imaginary dragons!

Suddenly the air crackled with heat,

smoke billowed all around,

and there stood something full of fire
and flame and a fight to be fought . . .

a real dragon!

The little knight had no
choice—it was too late to run—

so he **whooshed**

and **swooshed**   the sunflower sword.

It cut through the air like a fine silver blade,
but suddenly, as it swung near him,
the dragon saw what it was and . . .

. . . reached out to take it!

Could it be? thought the
dragon. Has this little
knight climbed to the top of Dragon Hill
to offer me a flower?

Could it be? thought the little knight. A
dragon might not be so fearsome after all?

Then the little knight and the dragon looked
at each other, and both began to smile.

So that's how it happened, as simply as that. From then on, they met each day on Dragon Hill and played much better games than fighting.

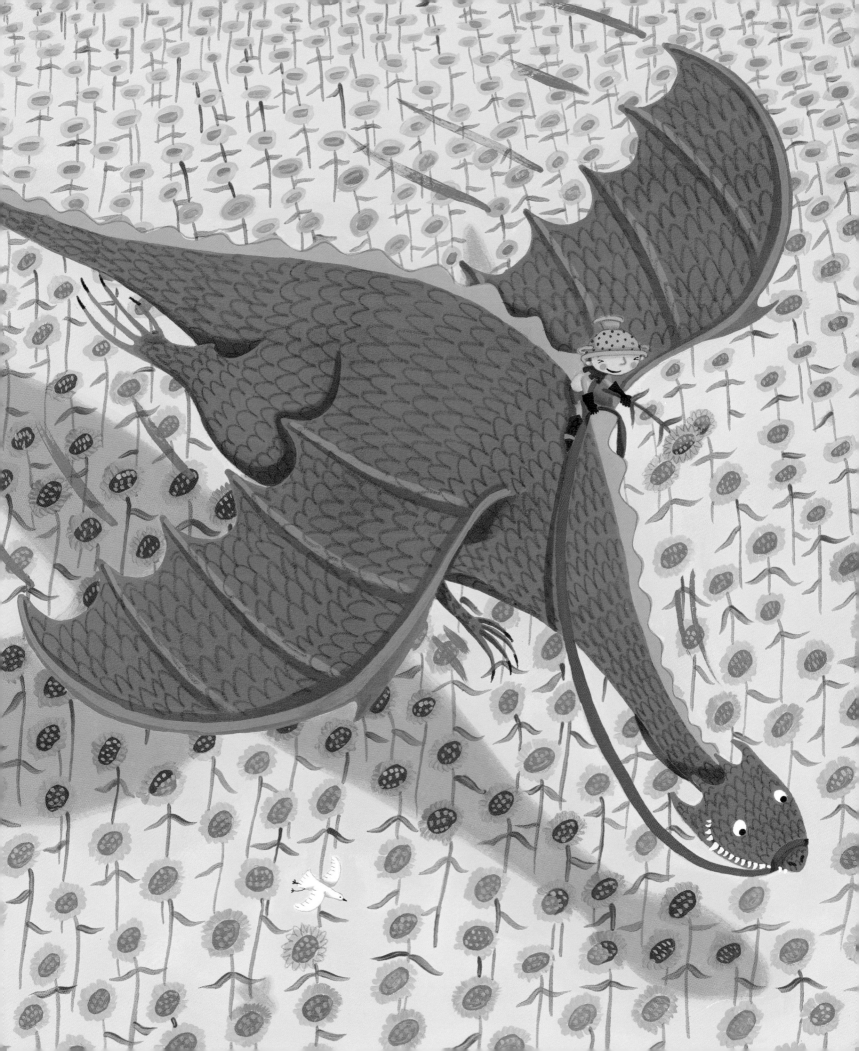

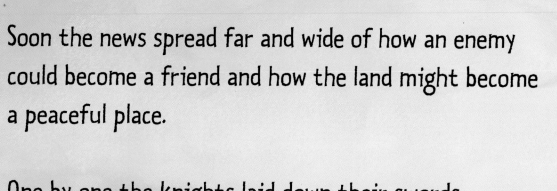

Soon the news spread far and wide of how an enemy
could become a friend and how the land might become
a peaceful place.

One by one the knights laid down their swords,
climbed to the top of Dragon Hill . . .

... and waited,

while the little
knight's mother
looked on and smiled.